Where is Binky Boo?

Where is

First published 2011 by Macmillan Children's Books
a division of Macmillan Publishers Limited
20 New Wharf Road, London N1 9RR
Basingstoke and Oxford. Associated companies throughout the world
www.panmacmillan.com
ISBN: 978-0-230-74845-3
Text and illustrations copyright © Chlöe Inkpen and Mick Inkpen 2011
Moral rights asserted. All rights reserved.
3 5 7 9 8 6 4
A CIP catalogue record for this book is available from the British Library.
Printed in Italy

Zoe and Beans

Chloë & Mick Inkpen

Binky Boo?

MACMILLAN CHILDREN'S BOOKS

Zoe loved Molly…

. . . but so did Beans.

It had become
a bit of a problem.
Ever since he'd lost
Binky Boo.

(This is Binky Boo)

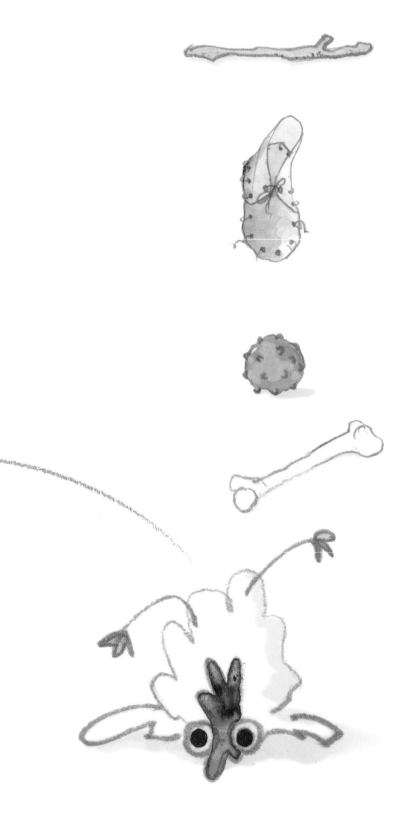

Beans wouldn't
fetch a stick.
He wouldn't fetch
his doggy shoe chew,
or his bobbly ball,
or his bone.
Boring!

Zoe even bought
him a special
squeaky chicken.
But he wasn't
interested.

He would **only**
fetch Molly.

And then he
wouldn't give her back.

Beans carried Molly
around **all** day.

He licked and chewed
and **slobbered** on her
as if she was his very own.

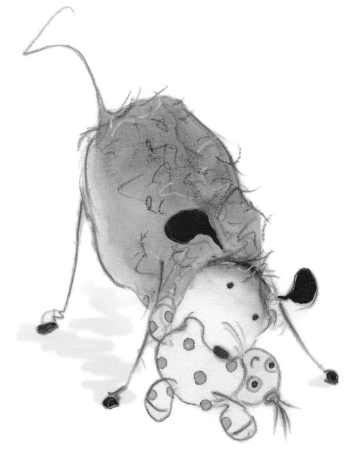

He even took her to the

park to meet his friends!

When Molly came home something awful had happened.
She smelled horrible!
Not like Molly at all!
Poo! (She smelled a bit like Binky Boo.)

Zoe couldn't cuddle her in bed that night.
'You're too stinky,' she explained.
'No offence.'

In the morning
Molly went straight in the
washing machine.
Zoe poured in an
entire box of
Big 'n' Bubbly,
just to be on the safe side.

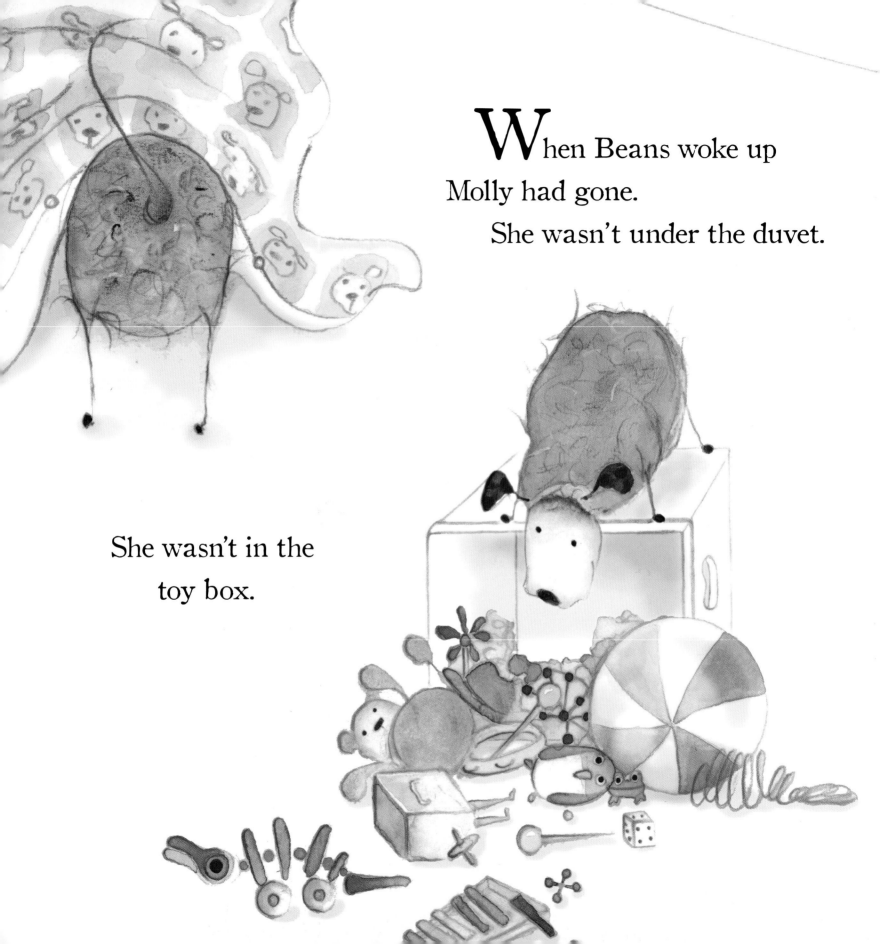

When Beans woke up
Molly had gone.

She wasn't under the duvet.

She wasn't in the
toy box.

Eventually he found her
dripping on the washing line.
But something awful had
happened.
She smelled horrible!
Not like Molly at all!
Poo!

Beans didn't like the
new Molly. He wouldn't lick her,
or chew her, or slobber on her.

He wouldn't have anything
to do with her.

Where is **Binky Boo?**
he thought.

wheeeeeeeeeeeeeeeeeeeeeeeeee

'Cheer up, Beans!'
Zoe whooped and
hollered, and jumped
up and down.

She whirled Molly
round and round and
threw her as far as she
possibly could.

Molly landed
plop!
in the sandpit.

'Fetch!' said Zoe.
But Beans wasn't impressed.
He was sulking.

'Fetch Beans! Fetch!'
Beans didn't move.

'Fetch!!!'

Beans looked at
Zoe and sighed.
Slowly he got up
and wandered up
the garden.

Suddenly Beans was barking!
Barking like mad!
'What is it Beans?'

Beans had found something exciting. Much more exciting than Molly.

A little woolly something sticking out of the sand.

A little woolly something with a familiar smell.

A little woolly something he had buried some time ago . . .

'What is it Beans?'

Sploof!

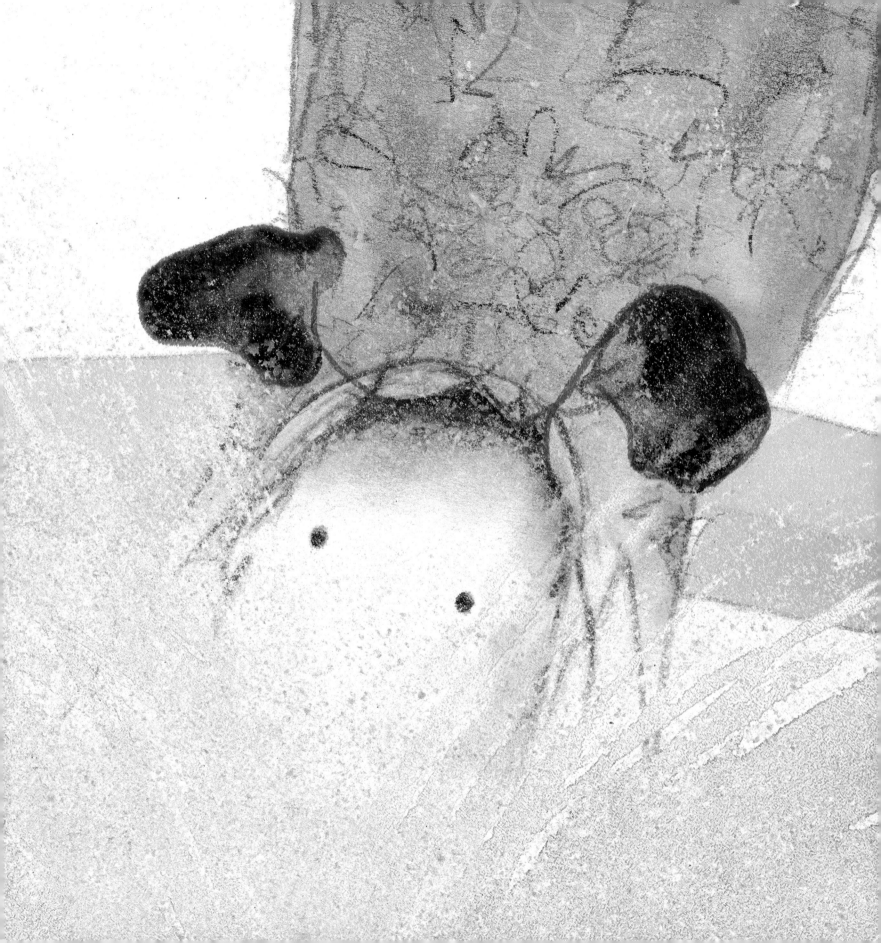

It's

BinkyBoo!